Rock Star
Road Trip

Maverick
Chapter Readers

'Rock Star Road Trip'
An original concept by Jenny Moore
© Jenny Moore 2022

Illustrated by Vicky Lommatzsch

Published by MAVERICK ARTS PUBLISHING LTD
Studio 11, City Business Centre, 6 Brighton Road,
Horsham, West Sussex, RH13 5BB
© Maverick Arts Publishing Limited February 2022
+44 (0)1403 256941

A CIP catalogue record for this book is available at the British Library.

ISBN 978-1-84886-862-5

www.maverickbooks.co.uk

This book is rated as: Lime Band (Guided Reading)

Rock Star
Road Trip

Written by
Jenny Moore

Illustrated by
Vicky Lommatzsch

Chapter 1

Lola looked at the calendar and grinned. A few weeks before, Dad had won tickets to see her favourite band, Boom Rabbit. Lola had been counting down the days ever since. But the long wait was finally over! When Boom Rabbit walked out on the stage at Rockson-on-Sea in a few hours' time, she and Dad would be right there in the front row!

There was just one problem. Lola's dad was a coach driver, and he had to take a group of pensioners to Rockson-on-Sea for a trip that day. This meant Lola would have to join them on the coach. Lola *hated* coaches—they always made her travelsick.

But she didn't mind feeling ill if it meant she got to see her favourite band. Once they'd dropped the pensioners at the beach, she and Dad would nip to the Rockson Arena for the lunchtime charity concert.

Lola really hoped they'd play 'Nowhere Road'. She'd been learning to play it on her own guitar and knew all the words.

In fact, Lola knew all the words to *every* Boom Rabbit song!

"I've got a one-way ticket to nowhere fast," she sang, as she put on her Boom Rabbit t-shirt and baseball cap. "Where every turn's a dead end and every stop's the last…"

Dad's face appeared round the door.

"*I've* got a steaming pot of porridge and a fresh cup of tea," he sang, adding his own silly words. "And I'm waiting for my daughter to have breakfast with me!"

Lola giggled. "No singing along at the concert today," she joked. "Otherwise they'll throw us out!"

"I'll do my best," said Dad. "But I can't promise not to sing on the coach. The Pensioners' Club love a good singalong. Once they get started with 'Ten Green Bottles' there's no stopping them!"

Oh no, thought Lola. *That's all I need… I'd better take my headphones!*

Chapter 2

Lola was feeling sick before they'd even reached the pick-up point. She sucked on a ginger travel sweet and tried to focus on the concert instead of the squirming feeling in her stomach. It would all be worth it once they got there.

"Here we go," said Dad as they swung round the roundabout and pulled up at the village hall.

Lola groaned.

"Don't worry," Dad added, patting her arm. "You'll feel better once we're on the motorway. A nice straight road—that's what you need."

Lola hoped he was right. What she *didn't* need were all the different flavours of perfume wafting past her nose as the pensioners headed for their seats. And she *really* didn't need the man behind her getting out his stinky egg sandwiches as soon as they set off.

Lola pulled out her headphones and put on her favourite Boom Rabbit playlist. Maybe some music would soothe her mind and settle her stomach. But it was no good. 'Nowhere Road' had only just started when a loud-voiced lady at the back of the coach suggested a singalong: "How about 'Ten Green Bottles'?"

"Let's make it a hundred green bottles," shouted someone else. "All together now... A hundred green bottles sitting on the wall..."

The noise of their singing drowned out the Boom Rabbits' lead singer, Paddy Gorr. By the time they reached eighty bottles, Lola was ready to scream.

"Please Dad," she begged. "Make them stop."

"Sorry, sweetheart," he said. "I'm just the coach driver. Don't worry," he added. "Only another seventy-nine verses to go after this one."

Chapter 3

Lola felt much better after a stop at the service station. Fresh air and a break from all the singing was just what she needed.

"Okay, sweetheart?" asked Dad, as she followed the pensioners back on board.

"Yes thanks," said Lola. "As long as that's the end of those green bottles!"

"Fingers crossed!" laughed Dad. "I'll just do a quick head count and we'll be on our way. Boom Rabbit rock show here we come!"

He counted up the pensioners. "Fifteen, sixteen... Wait, that's not right." Dad counted again. And again. "Oh dear," he frowned, "we seem to be missing someone."

"Where's Derek?" someone asked.

"He said he was heading back to the coach ages ago," replied someone else. "Maybe he got lost."

"Don't worry," said Dad, looking anxious. "He can't have gone far."

Everybody piled back off the coach to look for the missing passenger.

"Derek!" Lola shouted across the car park. What if they couldn't find him? What if they missed the concert? "Derek!"

"Derek," echoed the old lady next to her. "Where are you?"

After ten more minutes of frantic shouting, Lola was starting to panic. But a sleepy voice finally answered, "I'm here!" It was the man with the smelly egg sandwiches! "I'm sorry," he said, his cheeks flushed with embarrassment. "I got back on the wrong coach and fell asleep! Luckily the driver noticed she had an extra passenger and woke me up, otherwise I'd be on my way to Brightstone by now!"

Thank goodness for that, thought Lola, as everyone scrambled back on board. *Next stop Rockson-on-Sea!*

Chapter 4

The traffic was bad on the next stretch of motorway and Lola started worrying about missing the concert again. She felt more sick than ever now, thanks to Derek's smelly pickled onions. The singing had started again too. *Agghhh!*

The pensioners were just launching into 'I Do Like to be Beside the Seaside' for the fifteenth time, when there was a shrill cry from the back of the coach:

"HELP!"

Everyone stopped singing and turned round to look.

Derek dropped his lunchbox in shock, sending pickled onions flying everywhere.

"Are you okay?"

"What's wrong, Doris?"

"My purse is gone!" came the shrill reply.

"STOP THIS COACH AT ONCE!"

Lola frowned. *Stop the coach?* There was no time for that!

"It's a disaster!" cried Doris. "A calamity!"

"Don't worry, we'll help you look for it." Doris's friends undid their seatbelts and eased themselves onto the floor.

"Found it!" called a lady with round pink glasses. "Ew no, yuck! That's a pickled onion!"

"Back in your seats everyone please," called Dad. "I'll stop once we're off the motorway and you can look for it then."

"I can't wait that long!" wailed Doris. "It's got all my money in it. And my favourite photo of Bonzo."

"Who's Bonzo?" someone asked. "I thought your husband was called Albert."

"Bonzo's my dog," bawled Doris. "PLEASE," she begged, tipping her handbag upside down.

Tissues and toffees and dog treats fell out. "It's definitely not in my bag... I must have left it at the service station. We have to turn round now!"

No, no, no, thought Lola. *We have to keep going. We have to get to that concert!*

"Everyone stay calm," called Dad. "I'll stop as soon as it's safe and ring the service station to check if it's been handed in."

"Hurry," gasped Doris, "before I faint with worry."

Yes, hurry, thought Lola, willing the coach on faster and faster. *We don't want any fainting old ladies.*

"Here we go," said Dad at last, as he steered into a layby, sending stray pickled onions rolling across the floor. "I'm ringing them now, Doris. What does your purse look like?"

"Like this!" said Doris, waving a big red purse in the air. "Don't worry, everyone. It was in my coat pocket all along!"

Chapter 5

Time was ticking on and Lola was getting really worried now. *We can't miss the concert*, she thought, as the coach crawled along behind a tractor. *We just can't.*

"Don't worry," said Dad. "I'm sure the tractor will turn off soon." He paused. "Wait a minute... is that...? No, it can't be..."

Lola peered through the windscreen at a broken-down minibus up ahead. A tall, skinny man stood beside it, waving his arms at the passing traffic. "We haven't got time to stop and help," she said, before Dad got any ideas. "We need to keep going."

But it was too late. Dad was already slowing

down—as if they weren't going slowly enough already! "We can't just leave him there," said Dad. "We won't be able to enjoy the concert if we don't stop and help."

Lola groaned in despair. "There won't be any concert left to enjoy at this rate," she said. "It'll have finished by the time we get there."

Why did Dad have to be so kind and helpful all the time? She sank back into her seat with a loud sigh and pulled her Boom Rabbit cap down over her eyes in a sulk. She could hear Dad outside offering to give the man and his friends (and all their luggage) a lift to Rockson-on-Sea. That meant even more delay while Dad loaded up the strangers' stuff and found seats for them all. Lola put her headphones back on and turned her music up extra-loud to try and block out the panicked voice in her head: *We're going to miss the show! My one chance to see Boom Rabbit live and we're going to miss it!*

Lola didn't need to be able to see or hear to know they were finally on their way again though. The queasy feeling in her stomach was a giveaway. And so was the sound of a new singalong starting up behind her. Not even the loudest Boom Rabbit track could drown out the Pensioners' Club!

But wait a minute, what was that? Someone else had joined in the singing this time... Someone who sounded very familiar. Lola paused her music and took off her headphones to listen. *I know that voice*, she thought, pulling up her cap and twisting round in her seat to check she hadn't imagined it.

And there he was: Paddy Gorr himself, singing along with the pensioners and the other members of Boom Rabbit.

"Dad!" Lola gasped. "Do you know who that is?"

Dad winked at her in the rear-view mirror. "I certainly do! I told you we wouldn't be able to enjoy the concert if we didn't stop to help. There wouldn't even *be* a concert!"

Lola was too shocked to answer. The worst road trip ever had just become the *best* one ever.

Chapter 6

"I'm sorry I was so grumpy, Dad," said Lola, leaning forward in her seat to make herself heard over the singalong. "I'll try and be more kind and helpful like you next time."

"That's alright, sweetheart," Dad told her. "I knew it was only because you were worried about missing the show. No chance of that now though!"

"All thanks to you," Lola agreed. "I'd give you a big hug to say 'thank you' if you weren't driving the coach! I'll have to save it until we get to Rockson-on-Sea."

"Not much longer now." Dad pointed to a road sign up ahead. "Just time for a few hundred more verses of 'The Wheels on the Coach'."

Lola grinned. "Don't worry, I've got an idea." She turned round and waved her hands to get Paddy Gorr's attention. "Excuse me, Mr Gorr," she shouted down the coach. The pensioners stopped singing, to listen. "Would you be able to teach us one of your songs next? Something like 'Nowhere Road'. That's my favourite. I know all the guitar chords too!"

"I'd be honoured," said Paddy, with a big smile. The pensioners cheered.

"Will there be rapping?" asked Derek. "I'm a brilliant rapper!"

"And I know how to beatbox," added Doris. "My grandson taught me."

By the time the coach finally pulled into Rockson-on-Sea, everyone was singing along to 'Nowhere Road'.

"Great beatboxing, Doris!" said Paddy Gorr. "You're *all* brilliant. Thank you for stopping to help and making us feel so welcome. It's a shame you're going to the beach today or I'd invite you to the concert to say thank you."

"We can go to the beach any time," said

Doris. "I'd rather go to the concert."

"And me," agreed Derek.

"Me too," echoed the others.

Paddy grinned. "Excellent! I'll get the organisers to give you all backstage passes. How does that sound?"

It sounds brilliant, thought Lola. *Totally brilliant!*

★★★

It *was* brilliant. The band were even better live than Lola had imagined. Her ears thrummed to the music, and the pumping beat of the drums and guitars vibrating. The stage was alight with flashing colours and lasers as the band played all her favourite songs, one after the other, finishing with 'Nowhere Road'. The crowd went wild—clapping and cheering and stamping their feet. When Dad got a special shout-out from Paddy, for stopping to help, Lola was cheering louder than anyone.

"In fact, we'd like to thank all our new coach friends," added Paddy. "So we want to invite you to join the band on stage and help us sing 'Nowhere Road' one last time."

Lola thought she might burst with excitement. But there was still one more surprise to come.

"And I've got a spare guitar here," said Paddy, "if you'd like to join in with the chords, Lola."

"I'd *love* to," she said, feeling like a proper rock star as she jammed with her musical hero live on stage:

"I've got a one-way ticket to nowhere fast,

Where every turn's a dead end and every stop's the last,

Where every road sign's empty and there's nothing more to see,

But I'll drive this road forever as long as you're with me."

Discussion Points

1. How did Lola get tickets to see Boom Rabbit?

2. Why does Lola hate coaches?
a) She doesn't like the noise
b) She finds them boring
c) She gets travelsick

3. What was your favourite part of the story?

4. Who went missing at the service station?

5. Why do you think Lola got more and more frustrated during the trip?

6. Who was your favourite character and why?

7. There were moments in the story when Lola had to be **patient**. Where do you think the story shows this most?

8. What do you think happens after the end of the story?

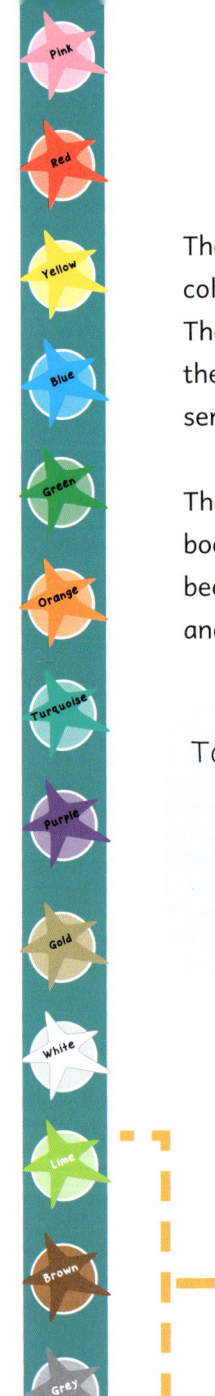

Book Bands for Guided Reading

The Institute of Education book banding system is a scale of colours that reflects the various levels of reading difficulty. The bands are assigned by taking into account the content, the language style, the layout and phonics. Word, phrase and sentence level work is also taken into consideration.

The Maverick Readers Scheme is a bright, attractive range of books covering the pink to grey bands. All of these books have been book banded for guided reading to the industry standard and edited by a leading educational consultant.

To view the whole Maverick Readers scheme, visit our website at

www.maverickearlyreaders.com

Or scan the QR code to view our scheme instantly!

Maverick Chapter Readers
(From Lime to Grey Band)

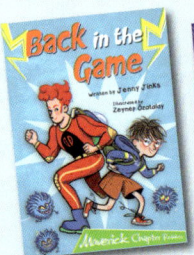
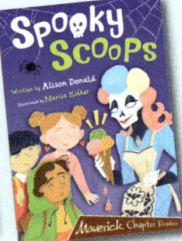
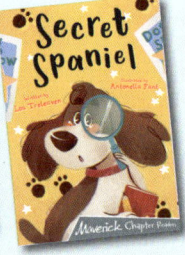